LADYBIRD BOOKS, INC.
Auburn, Maine 04210 U.S.A.
© LADYBIRD BOOKS LTD 1991
Loughborough, Leicestershire, England

Christmas Bear

Georgina Russell
illustrated by Jenny Press

Ladybird Books

A tear rolled down Sally's cheek as her mother switched off the bedroom light. It was Christmas Eve and Sally had forgotten to mail her letter to Santa Claus. She had found it stuffed in her jacket pocket.

How would Santa know what Sally really wanted? Maybe he'd forget her altogether!

Sally and her parents had still put out two mince pies and a glass of milk to welcome Santa. The red stocking hung ready at the foot of her bed as it did every Christmas Eve. But this year Sally was sure it would remain empty.

She sniffed miserably to herself as she drifted off to sleep....

*   *   *

A bright shape raced through the starry sky.
It was Santa Claus riding in his biggest sleigh, pulled
by his fastest reindeer!

The sleigh was filled with sacks of presents, neatly
sorted and labeled for children all over the world.

But in one of the sacks something was stirring....

A little paw appeared, and then another. Then two ears, followed by a furry head and a furry body.

It was a teddy bear...a very naughty teddy bear.

The sleigh made a sudden turn.
One second the teddy bear was safe
on the speeding sleigh, and the next he was
falling down, over and over and over.
He gave one shrill squeak, but Santa Claus heard
nothing except the rushing of the wind and the
jingling of the reindeer's bells.

Over and over Bear fell, toward white fields far below.
Down
      and down
            and down he went...

...until suddenly he landed in the snow-laden branches of
a fir tree.

"Ouch!" he cried as he slid through the prickly branches
and disappeared into a deep snowdrift.

All was still and silent and very, very cold.

Bear couldn't tell whether he was upside down or the right way up. It was some time before he pushed away the snow and found himself looking out into the night.

A little way off he saw a person dressed all in white.

"Aha!" said Bear. "*There's* someone who will help me."

He struggled to his feet and trudged through the snow, which as you can imagine seemed very deep to a little bear.

"Excuse me," he called out as he came closer. "Can you please tell me where I am?"

There was no answer from the person dressed in white.

Bear tried once more. "Excuse me," he said loudly. "Can you tell me where I am?"

Again there was no answer. The person in white didn't even look down to see who was talking.

"Well!" said Bear, turning away. "I hope all the people here aren't so rude!"

Bear was now feeling very cold and sorry for himself.
He wished he was safe and snug in Santa's sack.

He sighed and looked around. Not far off there was
a house. *And where there is a house,* Bear said to himself,
there will be people and warmth.

He walked around the house twice, trying to find a way in, but the door handles and windows were all too high for him to reach.

He was about to give up hope when a black cat came padding around the corner. It stopped and looked the little bear up and down, its fur bristling and its whiskers twitching. Then, deciding that bears were of no great interest, the cat turned and walked away.

The cat climbed up some steps to a closed door and then vanished completely. The last Bear saw of it was its tail disappearing through the unopened door.

"A magic cat!" thought Bear.

But he soon discovered that the cat had its own private cat-sized door. There in front of him was a hinged flap.

Bear reached up and pushed himself against it. The next thing he knew, he was tumbling head-first through the opening.

Bear thumped down onto a soft carpet. What bliss to be inside!

For a minute he lay still with his eyes shut, enjoying the warmth and comfort. Then he opened his eyes.

It was very dark. In front of him there was a staircase, and at the top he saw a dim light.

"It's time for a good snooze," Bear thought. He'd had enough adventures for a while.

Bear dragged himself up toward the light. He was out of breath when he pulled himself up the last step.

The light was coming from an open door. From inside, Bear could hear the sound of soft breathing.

He tiptoed to the door and nearly tripped over something lying just inside. It was a plate with two mince pies on it! Next to it was a small glass of milk.

Now Bear felt very hungry indeed. He sat himself down by the plate and ate steadily and happily until he had finished both pies.

"How kind of them to think of me!" Bear thought, gulping down the milk.

It was only then that he started to look around the room. In one corner there was a bed, and in it someone was sleeping peacefully.

"That's where I'd like to be," Bear whispered.

It wasn't easy getting up onto the bed, but he finally did it. A tired bear can be a very determined bear if he spots a comfortable place to sleep.

The effort was worth it. For what should he find at the end of the bed but a cozy red sleeping bag. It was just the right size!

In no time at all he had snuggled his way into it and had fallen fast asleep....

*   *   *

Sally opened her eyes. It was morning. Christmas morning!

But Sally's heart sank as she remembered her unmailed letter to Santa.

Had he brought her anything at all? She looked toward the door. The mince pies and the milk were gone!

Quickly, she crawled down to the bottom of the bed. The red stocking was no longer flat and empty. It was bulging. There really *was* something in it!

Bursting with excitement, she reached in and pulled out...a furry teddy bear!

Sally gazed at it wide-eyed. "But how could Santa have known you were exactly what I wanted?" she asked the little bear, thinking of the letter in her jacket pocket. This is what it said:

Was it Sally's imagination, or did the little bear seem to smile?